Ruby Kate's Scrumptious Tea Cake Party

Carol Hair Moore

Illustrated by Michael Harrell

Ruby Kate's Scrumptious Tea Cake Party

To order additional copies of this book:
Order online: www.iwishyouicecreamandcake.com
Phone orders: (850) 893-1514
Series: I Wish You Ice Cream and Cake Book 3

Inquiries should be addressed to:
CyPress Publications
P.O. Box 2636
Tallahassee, Florida 32316-2636
http://cypresspublications.com
lraymond@nettally.com

Library of Congress Control Number: 2011932507

ISBN: 978-1-935083-36-8

First Edition

Printed in the United States of America

Dedicated to my children's spouses.
Corbin Conway Moore
Charles Bass Reed (Chip)
Frank Sampson Shaw III
I love you with all my heart.

This is the story of a very special tea party.
Ruby Kate wanted to thank her loyal friends
for their kind ways of helping others.

1

Ruby Kate was a very beautiful Florida Black Bear.
She lived in the pine flat woods near the Crooked River
on the isle of St. James, Florida.

Her home was in the cavity of a very old scrub oak tree.

Each day she would put on her pretty apron and
sweep up her little house and yard.

Her Aunt Sissy taught her to be a good housekeeper.

She foraged for her food each day. This morning she would eat her breakfast of honey, acorns, nuts, and berries.

She has three special friends and neighbors who live near her. They are Frank the Gopher Tortoise, Katherine the Eastern Indigo Snake, and Franny the Florida Scrub Jay Bird.

Frank, the gopher tortoise, brought happiness to those who were sick.
He would visit his forest neighbors and find out their needs.

His strong shell was just right for the delivery of the items needed. Today he would deliver nuts to Walter Squirrel. Walter had the flu.

Katherine the Eastern Indigo Snake could not see well. She wore thick glasses and was always losing them.

She helped others by visiting
neighbors who were homebound.
She would read to them.
They would laugh joyfully
at the funny stories she
shared with them. She visited
Edgar Eagle today.

Franny the Florida
Scrub Jay Bird
sang beautiful songs.
She brought joy
as well as protection
to her friends
in the forest.

Franny was a large bird.
If she saw a hawk, she would
give an alarm call.
Everyone who could hear her
would dive for cover.
The three little mice, Mattox,
Sam, and Charlie, were thankful
for Franny. They were always
hiding from Murray Fox.

Hawks and foxes like to eat small forest creatures.

A delicious tea party would be a nice way for Ruby Kate to thank her friends and show her love for them. She planned her menu.

Ruby Kate invited her friends,
and included others in the forest.
She prepared the food and decorated
the party table and filled it with
all the delicious food.

She selected appropriate foods everyone would enjoy.
The most delicious were the scrumptious tea cakes.

The tea party day arrived!
Acorns, blackberries,
nuts, palmetto berries,
and of course
scrumptious tea cakes
filled the table.

19

All the creatures in the forest
enjoyed the tea party.

They danced and sang as the chirping of the crickets and the sparkle of the fireflies filled the cool summer night.

21

The sun was going to bed. The sky was turning a soft
and beautiful pink. Ruby Kate's friends thanked her
for honoring them in such a special way.

Showing appreciation for others brings joy to all.
Ruby Kate was a very happy Florida Black Bear.
She brought joy to those around her.

23

Host your own tea party and use
Ruby Kate's Scrumptious Tea Cake Recipe.
Celebrate your wonderful friends.

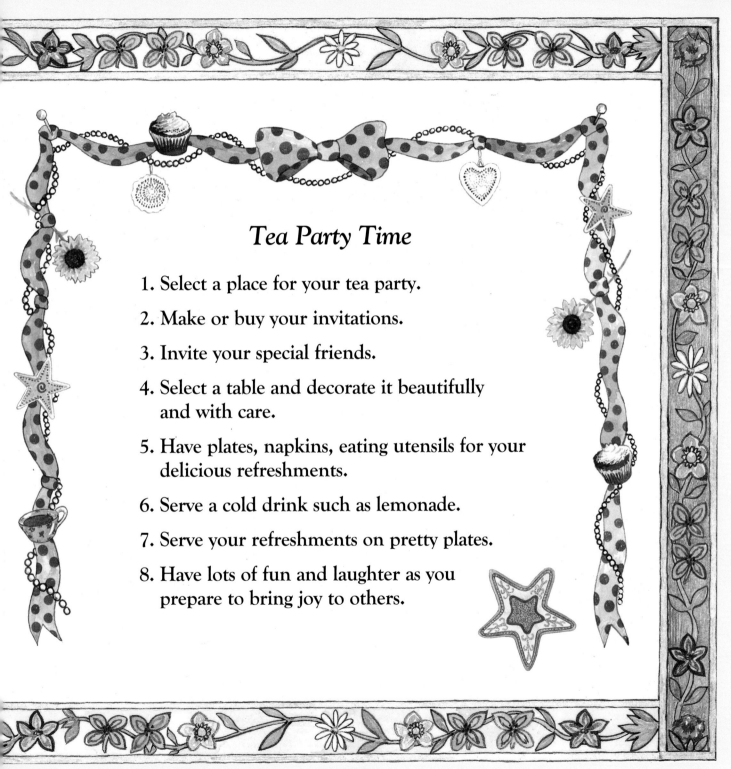

Tea Party Time

1. Select a place for your tea party.

2. Make or buy your invitations.

3. Invite your special friends.

4. Select a table and decorate it beautifully and with care.

5. Have plates, napkins, eating utensils for your delicious refreshments.

6. Serve a cold drink such as lemonade.

7. Serve your refreshments on pretty plates.

8. Have lots of fun and laughter as you prepare to bring joy to others.

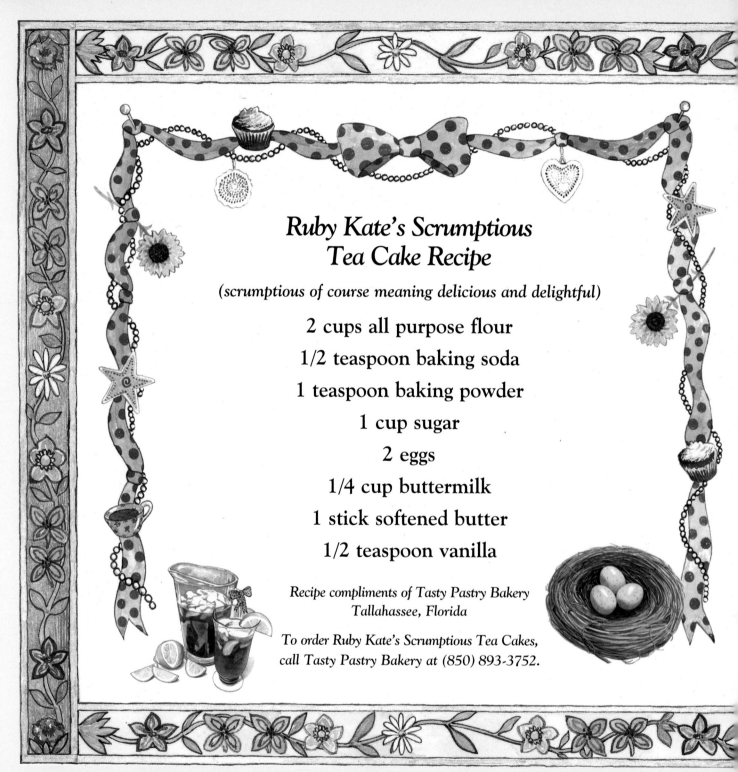

Ruby Kate's Scrumptious Tea Cake Recipe

(scrumptious of course meaning delicious and delightful)

2 cups all purpose flour

1/2 teaspoon baking soda

1 teaspoon baking powder

1 cup sugar

2 eggs

1/4 cup buttermilk

1 stick softened butter

1/2 teaspoon vanilla

*Recipe compliments of Tasty Pastry Bakery
Tallahassee, Florida*

*To order Ruby Kate's Scrumptious Tea Cakes,
call Tasty Pastry Bakery at (850) 893-3752.*

Preheat oven to 350 degrees.

Sift flour, baking soda and baking powder together.

Add the remaining ingredients.

Roll the dough on a floured surface (wax paper is nice).

Use heart shaped or round cookie cutters to cut out your cookies.
A bear cookie cutter would be nice, or cookie cutter shapes like
Ruby Kate's friends in the book.

Bake on a greased cookie sheet for 12 minutes.
Have a wonderful tea party!

Have enough refreshments so each friend can have two
or three desserts. Make everyone feel welcome and very loved.

Education Pages

Isle of St. James

Isle of St. James, or St. James Island, is the southeastern portion of Franklin County, Florida. Sixty thousand acres are bordered by Ochlocknee Bay and River, Crooked River, Carrabelle River, and the Gulf of Mexico. Better known for its barrier islands, St. George, St. Vincent, and Dog Island, Franklin County's sister island, St. James, appears to the unobservant traveler to be a part of the mainland since the rivers forming the island's north and west boundaries are located in sparsely populated or unpopulated areas.

The island includes Alligator Harbor, Alligator Point, Bald Point, St. Teresa, Lanark Village, St. James, and its lone city, Carrabelle. It remains a rural enclave populated with a limited number of full-time residents, an influx of summer visitors, and all manner of wildlife. Most of the island remains undeveloped and includes vast expanses of pine forest and scrub habitat. Historically residents subsisted by fishing, oystering, and crabbing. Tourism and second-home residents are an ever-increasing force, but the island still affords a welcome respite from today's fast-paced lifestyle.

FLORIDA

Crooked River

McIntyre

Wooded Swamp

Marsh

Wooded

OCHLOCKONEE BAY

Ochlockonee

Wooded Swamp

Lookout Tower

Corn Landing

Oyster Bay

Bald Pt.

Marsh

Carrabelle River

Wooded Swamp

Wooded Swamp

ISLE OF ST. JAMES

St. Teresa Beach

Wilson Beach

Stingray Pt.

Leonard's Landing

Oyster Pt.

Turkey Pt.

Peninsula Pt.

Alligator Harbor

Alligator Point

Southwest Cape

Lighthouse Pt.

Turkey Pt. Shoal

Grass

~ GULF OF MEXICO ~

Lanark Reef

Florida Black Bear

The Florida Black Bear has shiny black fur, a light brown nose, and stubby tail. The male may weigh as much as 500 pounds but averages around 300. Females average about 200 pounds. Black bears have good eyesight, an acute sense of smell, and excellent hearing.

Living mainly in forests, they are also common in scrub oak and sand-pine areas as well as forested wetlands. The bears are generally solitary except during mating season. Our Florida bears do not hibernate during the winter but become less active, and the female will "winter den" and go without food while giving birth to cubs.

Bears are omnivores, eating both plants and animals. Fish, berries, nuts, roots, grubs, dead meat (carrion), and some small animals are included in their diet, but plants make up the majority of what they eat. They like the food we humans eat, particularly our garbage. In bear-populated areas, care must be taken to protect garbage so bears will not become dependent on this food source and create interaction problems with humans.

Since the ban on hunting in 1994, the Florida bear population has increased significantly, and it is no longer considered to be a threatened species. Road-kills are the number one cause of bear deaths in Florida. The Apalachicola Forest and adjacent areas have one of the largest populations of black bears.

Eastern Indigo Snake

This nonvenomous, blue-black, smooth-scaled snake is considered to be the largest species native to North America. It may exceed 9 feet in length and has a glossy iridescent blackish-purple sheen. "Lord of the Forest" is the translation of the Latin name for the eastern indigo. The snake is an endangered species and is protected by the federal government as well as the State of Florida.

Most abundant in the sandhill communities of Florida and Georgia, the snake will frequent flat-woods, hammocks, riparian thickets and slash pine forests as well as other environments and will change habitats based on the season. In the winter they are often found in gopher tortoise burrows and will stay in the same burrow with the tortoise. Indigos are sometimes killed when gopher burrows are "gassed" in an effort to kill rattlesnakes. Snakes may range during the summer over as much as 275 acres.

The Eastern Indigo will eat any small animal it can overpower, including other snakes. It is immune to rattlesnake venom. It will eat turtles, lizards, small birds, frogs, fish, snakes, and other small animals. It is not poisonous to humans and will seldom bite even if picked up.

Eastern Grey Squirrel

The Eastern Grey Squirrel has predominantly grey fur, but can have a reddish color. It has a white underside and a bushy tail. The Eastern Grey, like all squirrels, has four fingers on the front feet and five on the back. When running (bounding), the tracks of the back feet may be ahead of the tracks of the front feet. The bounding stride can be two or three feet long.

Food includes tree bark, seeds, acorns, nuts, and some types of fungi. It is estimated that each squirrel makes several thousand caches of food each season and has a very accurate spatial memory for locating those hoards. Predators include humans, hawks, raccoons, cats, and others. They have a complex tag-team defensive system, involving distracting predators with vigorous shaking of their tails. Communication among squirrels involves vocalization and posturing. Vocalizations include squeaking like a mouse, a low-pitched noise, a chatter, and a raspy chant. The squirrel is one of the few mammals that can descend a tree headfirst. It does this by rotating its back legs 180 degrees to allow the sharp rear claws to hook into the bark.

Gopher Tortoise

Native to the southeastern United States, the gopher tortoise is a "keystone" species since its burrows provide shelter for 360 other animal species.

The tortoise's upper shell is yellowish or grayish brown with skin gray to dark brown. It has a big head and long front legs for burrowing. The hind legs are somewhat similar in appearance to those of an elephant. Most gopher tortoises are less than one foot long.

Most of the gopher's time is spent in its long burrow, which may be as long as 48 feet and almost 10 feet deep. They are solitary animals except during mating season. Gopher tortoises eat over 300 species of plants, mainly grasses and legumes, but also mushrooms and berries. Their water comes from the food they eat, and they usually only drink in times of extreme drought. The main predators of tortoise eggs are armadillos, foxes, skunks, raccoons, and alligators. The gopher tortoise matures at 10 to 15 years of age and may live to be 40 years old.

Florida Scrub Jay

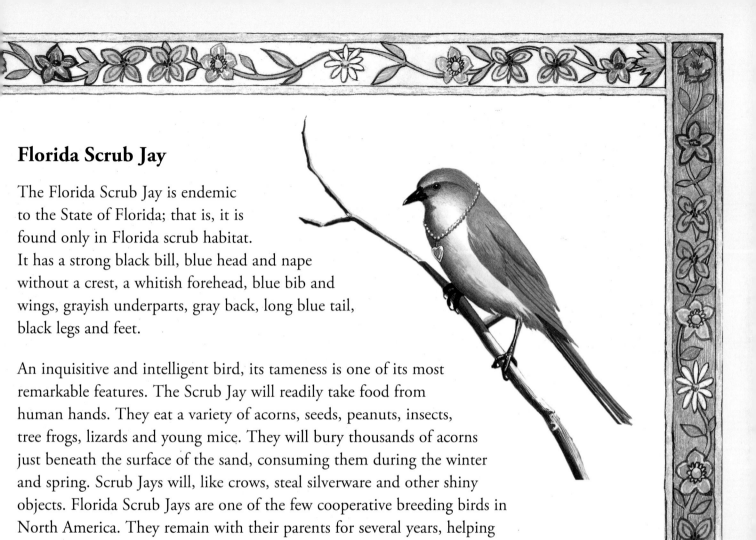

The Florida Scrub Jay is endemic to the State of Florida; that is, it is found only in Florida scrub habitat. It has a strong black bill, blue head and nape without a crest, a whitish forehead, blue bib and wings, grayish underparts, gray back, long blue tail, black legs and feet.

An inquisitive and intelligent bird, its tameness is one of its most remarkable features. The Scrub Jay will readily take food from human hands. They eat a variety of acorns, seeds, peanuts, insects, tree frogs, lizards and young mice. They will bury thousands of acorns just beneath the surface of the sand, consuming them during the winter and spring. Scrub Jays will, like crows, steal silverware and other shiny objects. Florida Scrub Jays are one of the few cooperative breeding birds in North America. They remain with their parents for several years, helping to rear the young, watch for predators and defend their territory. Families may range from 2 to 8 birds.

Bald Eagle

Bald Eagles are not actually bald. The name is derived from the older meaning of the word "white headed." It is the national bird and symbol of the United States of America and is the only sea eagle endemic to the United States. Threatened with extinction in the 1960s, the Bald Eagle has recovered to the point that it is no longer an endangered and threatened species.

An adult Bald Eagle is evenly brown with a white head and tail. Females are 25 percent larger than males. Wingspan may approximate 8 feet; however, the Florida Bald Eagles are somewhat smaller, with an adult male having a wingspan of slightly less than 6 feet.

The Bald Eagle's diet consists mainly of fish; however, mammalian prey includes rabbits, raccoons, beavers, and deer fawns. Also, ducks, gulls, geese, and other birds. Bald Eagles are considered apex predators, since they are not preyed upon in the wild.

Bald Eagles are sexually mature at 5 years of age, at which time they obtain the distinctive white head and tails. They are considered to be migratory; however, if food supply is plentiful, they will remain in the same range year-round. Mates for life, the eagles build the largest nests of any North American bird. One nest in Florida was found to be 20 feet deep, almost 9 feet across, and weighing almost 3 tons. Nests are used over and over. Florida has the largest population of Bald Eagles in the lower 48 states.

A powerful flier, the eagle can reach 43 miles per hour when gliding and flapping its wings and up to 99 miles per hour when diving. Lifespan in the wild is usually about 20 years, with the oldest living to about 30. An eagle in captivity lived to be 50 years old.

The Great Seal of the United States, which features the Bald Eagle, was adopted by Congress in 1782. Contrary to popular legend, there is no evidence that Benjamin Franklin ever supported the Wild Turkey as the symbol of the United States over the Bald Eagle.

Hawk

The Red-Tailed Hawk is one Florida's common hawks. It is a bird of prey and sometimes colloquially known as a "chicken hawk." It typically weighs 1.5 to 3.5 pounds, with a wingspan of 43 to 57 inches. It is legally protected in the United States, Canada, and Mexico. The majority of hawks used for falconry in the United States are Red-Tails. Markings may vary, but the red tail is uniformly brick red above and pink below.

When soaring or flapping its wings, it typically travels at 20 to 40 miles per hour, but when diving may exceed 120 miles per hour. Its diet is mainly small animals, but it will also prey on birds and reptiles. Eighty-five percent of the Red-Tail's diet consists of rodents. It hunts primarily from an elevated perch, swooping down on its prey. The Red-Tail's principal competitor is the Great Horned Owl. They also compete with each other for nest sites and may kill the young or destroy the eggs of the other. The feathers and other parts of the Red-Tail are considered sacred to many American indigenous people.

Florida Marsh Rabbit

The marsh rabbit is found in marshes and swamps. A strong swimmer, it is found only near water. Looking much like the eastern cottontail, it has smaller ears, legs and tail. Its body is blackish brown or dark reddish and its belly dingy brown, sometimes white. The leading edge of the ears has small black tufts. Hair color will change slightly during the year. One distinguishing feature is the underside of the tail is almost never white. The Florida Marsh Rabbit is sometimes confused with the larger, but distinct swamp rabbit. Adults weigh about 2.5 pounds.

Marsh rabbits feed on cattails, rushes and grasses as well as water hyacinth. They are most active nocturnally, hiding in thickets, logs, cattails and grasses during the day. When not hiding in logs and thickets, they will stay submerged in water with only their eyes and noses exposed and ears laid back flat. Although they can hop like other rabbits, they walk on all fours, placing each foot down alternately like a cat. Horned owls and hawks are major predators.

White Squirrel

In Sopchoppy and St. Teresa, Florida, there are rare colonies of white squirrels. These are not albino squirrels, but a mutation of the grey squirrel. These white squirrels have dark eyes and some will have grey or dark spots. They have successfully reproduced and the colonies are thriving.

White squirrels are found in other North Florida locations; however, some of those are identified as albinos. The true White Squirrel is rare and an object of interest and excitement for aficionados.

Lizard

One of the common lizards found in North Florida is the Green Anole. It is the only lizard native to the United States and is medium-sized with a long tail. It is sometimes called a chameleon since it can change its color from emerald green to brown or grey. Males have a pink throat fan. The toes have adhesive pads on the underside.

Green Anoles are easily tamed. They are active during the day and regularly bask head down on tree trunks, fence posts, decks or walls.

Red Fox

The red fox is commonly a rusty red, with white underbelly, black ear tips and legs and a bushy tail usually with a white tip. They resemble small dogs and usually weigh from 10 to 15 pounds. Probably not native to Florida except in North Florida Panhandle, they normally avoid heavily wooded areas.

Essentially a nocturnal animal, they are solitary hunters, feeding on insects, mollusks, blackberries, mice, rabbits, birds, eggs and fish. With an acute sense of hearing, they locate small mammals in thick grass, and jump high in the air to pounce on the prey.

A pair of foxes usually mate for life. Pups stay with their parents for about 6 months. Dens are burrows, sometimes borrowed from, or shared with, a gopher tortoise and are usually 20–40 feet long and 3–4 feet deep with multiple entrances.

Florida Mouse

The Florida Mouse is also known as the big-eared deermouse, the Florida deermouse and the gopher mouse. It is the only species of the genus podomys, which is the only mammal genus endemic to Florida. It is found in a limited area in Central Florida and one small area in the Florida Panhandle (Franklin County).

The mouse measures a little over 7 inches, has relatively large ears, brown to orange upper parts and white under parts. It often lives in tortoise burrows in passages constructed by the mouse. It has an odor similar to a skunk. The mouse favors dry environments as well as coastal scrub locations. Its diet consists of acorns, insects, seeds, nuts, other plant material, and vertebrates. Few wild individuals have a lifespan of over a year.

Carol is pictured presenting Busy Bumble Bee Rides The Waves *to the Florida Governor's Mansion Library.* Marvin the Magnificent Nubian Goat *and* Busy Bumble Bee Rides The Waves *are read to children visiting the Library.*

Carol has had a love for children and animals all of her life. Each of the six books in her series, "I Wish You Ice Cream and Cake," is designed to educate and give the children a life lesson. *Marvin The Magnificent Nubian Goat, Busy BumbleBee Rides The Waves,* and her newest book, *Ruby Kate's Scrumptious Tea Cake Party* are filled with family memories and wonderful life lessons, and each is beautifully illustrated by Michael Harrell.

"Ruby Kate" is named for Carol's grandmothers, Ruby Strickland and Kate Hair. The families have been in Live Oak, Florida, since the 1850s. Ruby served two terms as mayor of Live Oak. She also served as delegate from Florida to the Democratic National Convention in 1936 and was vice-chair of the Florida delegation. Kate was a loving grandmother who wore purple, even her hats and shoes, and lived in a big old "grandmother's" house. Carol shared lots of tea parties with her grandmothers, Ruby and Kate.

Carol received her B.S. Degree in Elementary Education from Florida State University. She taught second grade in Gainesville, Florida, while her husband Ed finished law school at the University of Florida.

Carol and Ed live in Tallahassee and enjoy their three children, the children's spouses, and their seven grandchildren. Church, family, friends, music, gardening, and writing are Carol's favorite pastimes.

After being on the endangered species list, the Florida Black Bear has made a strong comeback in North Florida, especially in the Panhandle where Carol's family has a home on the Gulf of Mexico.

As we learn to appreciate the Black Bear, remember not to feed them, to leave trash and garbage in protected areas, and never to approach a bear, particularly one with a cub.

Have a wonderful Tea Party and make all your dear friends feel special and loved. Ruby Kate loves her friends and found a special way to honor them.

Illustrator, Michael Harrell

Michael Harrell is a native of Tallahassee, Florida. He received a B.F.A. from the University of Georgia in 1989.

Harrell's seascapes and landscapes paintings can be found in private and corporate collections throughout the U.S. and abroad.

His oils and watercolors have been featured in many national publications, including *American Artist Watercolor* magazine, *American Art Collector*, and *The Artist's Magazine*. More than a dozen top galleries represent Harrell's work and, in 2004, *The Artist's Magazine* listed Michael Harrell as one of the top 20 artists in the United States to watch.

Michael Harrell's clients have included American Express, Paramount Pictures, Seaside, and the Mystic Seaport Museum.

Sparkle like the Stars ~ Shine like the Moon
Be Warm like the Sun